Join the **Rainbow Magic Reading Challenge!**

Read the story and collect your fairy points to climb the
Reading Rainbow at the back of the book.

For every child who dreams of adventure

Special thanks to
Rachel Elliot

ORCHARD BOOKS

First published in Great Britain in 2018 by The Watts Publishing Group

1 3 5 7 9 10 8 6 4 2

© 2018 Rainbow Magic Limited.
© 2018 HIT Entertainment Limited.
Illustrations © Orchard Books 2018

A CIP catalogue record for this book is available from the British Library.

ISBN 978 1 40835 077 5

Printed and bound in Great Britain by CPI Group (UK) Ltd, Croydon, CR0 4YY

MIX
Paper from
responsible sources
FSC® C104740

The paper and board used in this book are made from wood from responsible sources

Orchard Books
An imprint of Hachette Children's Group
Part of The Watts Publishing Group Limited
Carmelite House, 50 Victoria Embankment, London EC4Y 0DZ

An Hachette UK Company
www.hachette.co.uk
www.hachettechildrens.co.uk

Ellen
the Explorer
Fairy

by Daisy Meadows

ORCHARD

www.rainbowmagic.co.uk

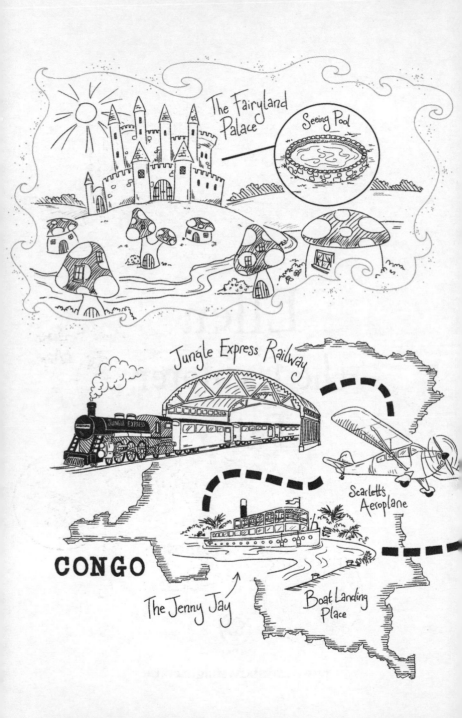

Contents

Story One:
The Felt Flower

Chapter One: All Aboard   11
Chapter Two: News From Fairyland   19
Chapter Three: Cabin 13   31
Chapter Four: A Messy Cabin   41
Chapter Five: A Brave Fairy   49

Story Two:
The Questing Compass

Chapter Six: Up and Away   59
Chapter Seven: Problems in Fairyland   67

Chapter Eight: Protect the King and Queen   77
Chapter Nine: Fog on the River   87
Chapter Ten: A Little Help from a Crocodile   97

Story Three:
The Mighty Magnifying Glass

Chapter Eleven: The Lion, the Eagle and the Star   111
Chapter Twelve: Ellen Returns   119
Chapter Thirteen: A Hopeless Search   125
Chapter Fourteen: The Magic of Friendship   135
Chapter Fifteen: Lost and Found   145

Jack Frost's Spell

I've followed Ellen up and down,
And left and right, and round and round.
That silly fairy's found no treasure.
It's like she's travelling for pleasure!

I've got more exciting dreams
Than hiking over rocks and streams.
I'll take that fairy's magic things,
And be as rich as fifty kings!

Story One:
The Felt Flower

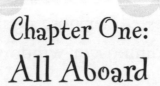

Chapter One:
All Aboard

"I've never had breakfast on a train before," said Rachel Walker. "It makes everything taste extra yummy."

She still couldn't believe that they were halfway around the world. It was only a day since they had left Wetherbury and boarded an aeroplane, but it felt like

longer. Now they were sitting on a train, speeding towards the Congo jungle.

Rachel pressed her nose against the glass of the dining-car window. The

famous Jungle Express train was speeding across a vast, flat savannah. She could see mountains in the far distance, and blue-white clouds swirling around their peaks. Rachel turned and smiled at her best

friend, Kirsty Tate.

"I still can't believe that we're really here," said Kirsty. "My mum told me that the Jungle Express is one of the most famous trains in the world."

Rachel nodded and picked up a teaspoon to stir her cup of hot chocolate.

"Even the teaspoons are engraved with the Jungle Express emblem," she said.

The girls smiled at each other and sipped their drinks. They were the best hot chocolates either of them had ever tasted.

"Your cousin Margot is so lucky," said Kirsty. "She's only a year older than us, but she has been to some of the most amazing places on the planet."

"That's because Aunt Willow is such a famous explorer," said Rachel. "Every

school holiday, she and Margot go
adventuring together. We hardly ever see
them. Last year they spent the whole
summer holiday in the Amazon rainforest.
Dad says that the harder a place is to get
to, the more Aunt Willow likes it. And this
time, we actually get to
join them."

"Tell me all
about it again,"
said Kirsty with
a wriggle of
excitement.

"Aunt Willow
has been trying to
find the Lost City of
the Congo for as long
as I can remember," said Rachel. "Now
she thinks she has found the map that

will lead her there. She said it will be the discovery of a lifetime. We have to take the train to the station on the edge of the Congo jungle and meet an aeroplane that will fly us across to the river. We'll take a boat down the river to a landing place, and then trek to the Lost City."

Kirsty leaned forward over the white tablecloth, her eyes sparkling.

"It's so thrilling," she whispered. "I'm not used to such incredible things happening in the human world."

The girls smiled at each other, thinking

15

about the many magical adventures
they had shared with their friends in
Fairyland. At that moment, the train
started to slow down, and then stopped
with a jerk. Teacups rattled in their
saucers, and the dining-car waiter lost his
balance and wobbled.

"Why are we stopping?" Kirsty asked,
looking out at the empty plain that

stretched around them. "This isn't a station."

"The driver seems to be having some trouble with the route this morning," said the waiter. "I expect he's stopping to check that he is on the right track."

Rachel frowned.

"But surely he has done this journey lots of times before?" she asked.

The waiter just shrugged and went to greet some new customers. Seconds later, the train jerked and then set off again. Kirsty took a bite of toast.

Suddenly, the teacup on the saucer next to Kirsty rattled. She looked at it in surprise.

"Are we stopping again?" she asked.

"No," said Rachel in a breathless
whisper. "Look at the cup, Kirsty – it's
glowing."

She reached out and turned the teacup
the right way up. A tiny fairy was
waving up at them from inside.

"Hello," she said in a cheerful voice.
"I'm Ellen the Explorer Fairy."

Chapter Two:
News from Fairyland

Ellen had bright green eyes, and her brown hair hung over her shoulders in two loose plaits. She looked ready for adventure in her checked shirt, blue trousers and sturdy walking boots.

"It's great to meet you, Ellen," said Kirsty. "But tell me, how did you know where to find us?"

"I didn't," said Ellen with a laugh. "This must be my lucky day. You see, Jack Frost and his goblins are on this train, and I'm trying to find them. I recognised you both as soon as I saw you. Everyone in Fairyland knows who you are."

Rachel and Kirsty felt their cheeks getting hot. Ellen was talking as if they

were famous, but they just felt lucky to
have met the fairies, and to have been
able to help them. Jack Frost loved
making trouble, but the girls and the
fairies had always managed to stop him
when they teamed up.

"Why is Jack
Frost on the
train?" Rachel
asked. "Is he
up to mischief
again?"

Ellen nodded.

"I was exploring
one of the furthest corners of Fairyland,"
she said. "It was exciting, because no one
had visited it for years. I thought I was
alone. But Jack Frost had decided that he
wanted to become an explorer himself,

and he was following me. Of course, he wasn't interested in finding out more about our amazing world, or meeting new people. He just wanted to find lost treasure and become rich and powerful. He was planning to steal anything that I found."

"Oh, that mean Jack Frost," said Kirsty, frowning. "Why does he always have to spoil everything?"

"He didn't understand that I wasn't searching for anything in particular," Ellen went on. "I was just adventuring and exploring. He got fed up with waiting for me to lead him to treasure, so he got his goblins to steal my magical objects while I was asleep in my tent."

"How awful," said Rachel.

"I have tracked him from Fairyland to the human world," said Ellen, looking determined. "I won't let him get away from me. I know that he and his goblins are somewhere on this train, and they have my magical objects. I have to get them back – will you help me?"

"Of course," said the girls together.

Ellen flashed them a dazzling smile.

"I have three magical objects," she said. "The seeking scroll helps people

23

remember directions. The questing compass makes sure they stay focused on their mission. And the mighty magnifying glass helps them to see things clearly."

"Talking of seeing things clearly, I can see my aunt and cousin coming this way," said Rachel. "Hide, Ellen!"

Quick as a flash, Ellen zoomed under a lock of Rachel's hair.

"We have to search the train," she whispered.

Rachel nodded as she waved to Aunt Willow and Margot.

"Good morning, girls," said Aunt Willow. "You must have got up early."

"We didn't want to miss a single moment," said Kirsty.

The waiter came over with a pot of tea for Aunt Willow, a cup of hot chocolate for Margot, and plates of hot buttered toast.

"Show them the map, Mum," said Margot, bouncing up and down excitedly in her seat.

Smiling, Aunt Willow took out a small leather case. She opened it, and the girls leaned forward. A thin piece of paper lay inside, faded with age. "I found this map in an old chest, hidden in a forgotten attic," said Aunt Willow. "If I'm right, it will lead us to the Lost City."

She pointed to a cluster of green trees on the map.

"I think this is the jungle," she said. "The blue line must be the river, and these yellow tracks show how to reach the site of the Lost City. I've dreamed of

finding it all my life. I can hardly believe that my dream might actually come true."

She took out a modern map and opened it across the table.

"This shows exactly where we have to go," said Aunt Willow. "You see, the plane will take us north – no – that can't be right. What's the opposite of west?"

"East?" said Kirsty in surprise.

"Yes, of course, silly me," said Aunt Willow in a brisk voice. "So as I was saying, the plane will take us east, and then we will meet the boat and travel south to the landing place."

"North, I think, Mum," said Margot.

"Is it?" said Aunt Willow. "But north is downwards, isn't it?"

"No, that's west," said Margot. "Or is it east?"

Rachel and Kirsty exchanged a worried glance. Aunt Willow had travelled around the world many times. Why was she suddenly getting confused about directions?

"This is because the seeking scroll is missing," Ellen whispered to Rachel. "Without it, no one can remember directions or read maps properly. We have to find Jack Frost — fast."

Chapter Three:
Cabin 13

Rachel took Kirsty's hand and they stood up together.

"We're really looking forward to the adventure, Aunt Willow," said Rachel. "We've got a few things to do now, so we'll see you later."

The girls left the dining car and tiptoed along the narrow train corridor, stopping

to put their ears against each cabin door.

"Listen out for squawks," Ellen whispered. "Goblins can never keep quiet for long."

The girls listened carefully, but they heard nothing that sounded like goblins.

"I wonder if they could be hiding in the luggage car," said Kirsty suddenly. "Jack Frost knows how loud they are — he might try to keep them away from human beings."

In the third carriage, they met one of the cabin stewards hurrying along the corridor towards them.

"Excuse me," said Rachel. "Could you tell me where the luggage car is?"

"Yes, of course," said the steward, smiling. "Um ..."

His smile faded and he looked confused.

"Is it near the back of the train or the front?" Kirsty asked.

"Well, it's definitely somewhere on the train," said the steward. "I think ..."

Rachel and Kirsty felt sorry for him. They knew that he had forgotten the

way because the seeking scroll was missing. They thanked him and carried on down the corridor, listening at each door. But when they reached the last carriage, they still hadn't heard a single squawk.

"What are we going to do now?" asked Rachel.

"Look," said Kirsty.

She pointed at a door at the end of the corridor. It was labelled 'luggage car'.

"It's our last hope," said Rachel.

Slowly, she turned the handle and opened the door. The noise hit them at once. Six goblins were leaping around on trunks and suitcases, dangling from the ceiling and squawking, yelling and whooping in delight. Some bags and boxes had been opened, and people's clothes and belongings were scattered

around the luggage car. Some of the goblins were even wearing the clothes. Rachel and Kirsty stared at the mess in horror.

"HUMANS!" squealed a small goblin with a high-pitched voice. "And a pesky fairy."

All six goblins froze on the spot. Then a goblin in a spotted silk tie jabbed his finger at Rachel and Kirsty.

"I know them," he told the other goblins. "They're those interfering humans who are always spoiling our fun. Jack Frost's going to be

furious when he finds out."

"Ooh, let's go and tell him," said the squeaky-voiced goblin.

The goblins made a rush for the window and pushed their way out, elbowing each other in the face.

"Please, stop!" cried Rachel. "That's very dangerous. You should never climb out of a moving train."

But the goblins took no notice. They scrabbled over each other and clambered up to the roof. Seconds later, the girls heard thudding footsteps above.

"We can follow the sound of their feet," Kirsty said.

The goblins thundered along the roof of the train like a herd of elephants. Rachel and Kirsty ran along the corridor below, trying to keep up. Ellen flew ahead of them. Then the footsteps stopped abruptly.

"Cabin number thirteen," said Ellen, looking at the door beside them. "I wonder if Jack Frost's in here."

They could hear muffled, angry voices inside the cabin.

"The goblins must have climbed in through the window," said Rachel.

"I bet this is where he's keeping the magical objects," added Kirsty. "But how are we going to get them?"

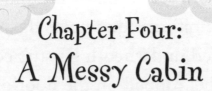

Chapter Four:
A Messy Cabin

"I've got an idea," said Rachel. "Ellen, can you use your magic to disguise us as cabin stewards? Maybe we can make Jack Frost leave the cabin so we can search for the magical objects."

"Good thinking," said Ellen.

She waved her wand, and instantly the girls were dressed in smart burgundy-and-gold uniforms and peaked caps. Ellen darted underneath Kirsty's cap, and then Rachel rapped on the door of cabin number thirteen.

"Who is it?" said a grumpy voice from inside the cabin.

"We're the cabin stewards," Rachel replied.

There was a scuffling sound, and then the door opened a crack. Jack Frost's nose poked out and his beady eyes peered at Rachel and Kirsty. They held their breath. Would he see through their disguise?

"What do you want?" he snapped.

"Breakfast is almost finished," said Kirsty truthfully. "You'll have to hurry if you want something to eat."

At once, Jack Frost flung open the door. He was wrapped in a long dressing gown of blue silk.

"Come on," he barked over his shoulder. "No dawdling."

He pushed past Rachel and Kirsty

and swaggered down the corridor towards the dining car. The six goblins pranced out of the cabin in single file. Each of them was swathed in a green silk dressing gown with a matching nightcap. One was even wearing a false moustache.

"Let's find my magical objects before they come back," said Ellen.

She swooped into the cabin, and Rachel and Kirsty slipped in after her. The beds were unmade, and clothes, papers and empty sweet wrappers were scattered all

over the floor.

"This isn't going to be easy," said Kirsty.

Rachel, Kirsty and Ellen searched every nook and cranny, but they couldn't find the magical objects anywhere.

"He must be carrying them with him," said Rachel to Ellen. "Let's go to the dining car and see if we can get them back."

Ellen hid under the peak of Rachel's

cap, and they left the cabin. When they reached the dining car, they saw that Aunt Willow and Margot had already gone. Jack Frost was busy shouting at the waiter.

"I don't want toast, you nincompoop!" he yelled. "I want a fresh tomato cut into little pieces with all the seeds taken out, orange juice with no bits, and six crumpets in the shape of goblins – now!"

There were a few other people in the dining car. They were all shaking their heads and tutting.

"Oh no," said Rachel. "He's spoiling the journey for everyone."

"It's our fault," said Kirsty. "We sent him here so we could search his cabin."

"We have to try to get him away from the other passengers," said Rachel.

Kirsty looked down at her steward's uniform and had an idea. Quickly, she scurried over to Jack Frost and bent down to whisper in his ear.

"Excuse me, sir," she said. "I think that someone is searching your cabin."

To her surprise, Jack Frost smirked and patted his dressing-gown pocket.

"They won't find anything," he said.

The goblins sniggered, and Kirsty felt a thrill of excitement. Jack Frost didn't suspect that they had found him out. Were they about to get Ellen's magical objects back after all?

Chapter Five:
A Brave Fairy

Jack Frost rose to his feet, and Kirsty darted back to Rachel and Ellen.

"I think the magical objects are in his pocket," she whispered, pulling them out into the corridor. "How are we going to get them?"

Jack Frost strode out of the dining car, and suddenly the train jerked to a stop.

Everyone fell down with a bump, and the
goblins starting yelling and squealing.

"Get off me, you nincompoop!"
bellowed Jack Frost, shoving an unlucky
goblin sideways.

"The driver must still be having trouble
with directions," said Rachel.

In all the confusion, Ellen zoomed out from under Rachel's hair and dived into Jack Frost's dressing-gown pocket.

"She's so brave," Kirsty whispered. "If Jack Frost catches her, he'll lock her up in his castle."

Jack Frost and the goblins were still scrambling to their feet. Jack Frost used two of the goblins to pull himself up, which knocked them down again. The corridor was a tangle of thin, knobbly goblin legs and green silk dressing gowns.

"Get up, you fools," Jack Frost hissed at them.

He pulled the goblins up and shoved them ahead of him, grumbling at them all the way down the corridor. As they walked away, Ellen darted out of Jack Frost's pocket and back towards Rachel

and Kirsty, who jumped to their feet.

"Did you find something?" Rachel asked, hardly daring to hope.

A huge smile lit up Ellen's face and she held out a cream-coloured scroll, fastened with a red flower seal.

"It's my seeking scroll," she said. "The questing compass and the mighty magnifying glass weren't there, but I am so happy that I can take the seeking scroll

back to Fairyland."

Rachel and Kirsty cheered and hugged each other. Still smiling, Ellen waved her wand and changed them back into their own clothes.

"Thank you both for helping me," she said. "I'm taking the seeking scroll back to Fairyland now. Will you help me again? Jack Frost still has my other magical objects."

"We'd be delighted to help," Kirsty told her. "We don't want to let Jack Frost's plans interfere with any more of our journey."

Ellen waved and disappeared, leaving a few sparkles of fairy dust fading in the air.

"Let's go and find Aunt Willow," said Rachel. "I want to make sure that her sense of direction is back to normal."

They found Aunt Willow in her cabin, poring over her maps.

"We'll be arriving at the jungle station soon," she told the girls. "A splendid Congo explorer called Scarlett should be waiting for us with her aeroplane. She'll take us east to the river, and from there we'll meet the boat and head north to the landing place."

The girls were happy to hear Aunt Willow describing the directions so clearly. The seeking scroll was working properly again.

Suddenly, they heard a distant roar, followed by a crash.

"Goodness, what was that?" asked Aunt Willow.

The girls exchanged an amused glance. They felt sure that it was the sound of Jack Frost realising that he had lost the seeking scroll, but they couldn't tell Aunt Willow that. Rachel bent down and gave her aunt a kiss.

"I expect it's all part of our adventure," said Rachel. "Thank you for inviting us along, Aunt Willow. We can't wait to find out what's going to happen next!"

Story Two:
The Questing
Compass

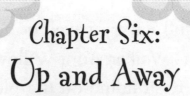

Chapter Six:
Up and Away

"Goodbye, Jungle Express!" called Rachel and Kirsty at the tops of their voices.

The famous train started to move away from the jungle station. The conductor leaned out of a carriage window and waved to them.

"Goodbye," he called. "See you

tomorrow for the return journey. Good luck!"

Rachel and Kirsty waved goodbye. Mr and Mrs Walker, Aunt Willow and Margot were standing on the platform beside them. Everyone was carrying a rucksack.

"That's odd," said Aunt Willow, looking confused. "Why did the conductor wish us good luck?"

Mr and Mrs Walker looked at each other and shrugged. Margot frowned.

"It's on the tip of my tongue," she said.

Rachel and Kirsty exchanged a worried glance.

"We're on our way to the Lost City of the Congo, remember?" Rachel said to her aunt in a gentle voice. "We're going to catch a plane and a boat, and then

follow your map."

"That's it," said Margot.

"Of course," said Mrs Walker with a laugh. "Silly me, how could I have forgotten?"

Rachel and Kirsty knew why she had forgotten. Without Ellen's questing compass, no adventurers would be able to stay focused on their mission.

Aunt Willow handed a piece of paper to Rachel.

"Could you read this out for me?" she said. "It's all the details of our journey. It all seems a bit foggy in my mind, and it would help to hear someone else read it out loud."

"Of course," said Rachel. "It says that we have to meet an explorer called Scarlett, and she will fly us across the jungle in her plane. When we reach the river, we will meet a boat, which will take us down the river to a landing place."

"Oh yes, I remember now," said Aunt Willow, taking the paper back and folding it up. "Let's go and find Scarlett."

"I've never seen a train station like this before," said Kirsty as they walked

towards a little gate at the end of the platform. "There's just one platform and no one is on duty."

"The Jungle Express is the only train that uses it," said Aunt Willow.

She led them through the little gate, and they stepped on to a short runway, surrounded by thick jungle. A small, white aeroplane was waiting there, with a woman leaning against it. She was wearing jeans, a blue shirt and a pair of brown cowboy boots. Her red hair was

piled high on her head and mirrored
sunglasses hid her eyes.

"Right on time," she said, striding
towards them. "Put your bags in the back
and let's go."

"She makes it sound as ordinary
as getting into a car," Rachel said in
amazement.

Aunt Willow laughed.

"It is that ordinary to Scarlett," she said.
"She's been flying planes over the Congo
and leading expeditions here since before
you were born."

She shook Scarlett's hand.

"It's good to see you again, Scarlett,"
said Aunt Willow. "We're all looking
forward to this ride. I hope you'll be able
to tell us a bit about the jungle on the
way."

"No problem," said
Scarlett. "Hop in."

Rachel and Kirsty
climbed up the steps
into the plane. There
was a single row of
seats on the left and
another on the right, with

a narrow aisle between them. The back
two seats were close together, and the
girls raced to sit in them.

"This is going to be so much fun," said
Rachel.

When everyone was sitting down
and strapped in, Scarlett did a quick
safety check. Then she took her place
and started the plane. It hurtled down
the runway and the girls bounced up
and down in their seats, giggling with

excitement. The nose of the plane lifted into the air and they rose up over the tall jungle trees.

"We're off!" cried Aunt Willow. "Next stop, adventure!"

Chapter Seven:
Problems in Fairyland

Riding in a small plane was bumpy, exciting and noisy. The girls had to shout if they wanted to speak to each other. If they spoke in their normal voices, they couldn't even hear themselves talking.

Aunt Willow was sitting in front of Rachel, her hair bouncing up and down. The plane tilted sideways, and they went

round in a circle.

"If you look down to the left, you'll see a circle of bare ground among the trees," said Scarlett. "That's a mysterious monument. No one knows who built it or how many years it's been there."

The plane kept going round in circles, and Margot groaned.

"I'm starting to feel a bit funny," she said.

"I think the questing compass is making Scarlett forget where she's supposed to be going," said Kirsty.

"Scarlett, which way is the boat?" asked Rachel, trying to remind her about their journey.

"Oh yes," said Scarlett, giving her head a shake.

She got the plane back on course, but

before long they were going around in circles again.

"There's a herd of elephants to your right," said Scarlett.

It was lovely to see the elephants, but after they had disappeared, Scarlett kept circling above. No one except the girls seemed to think it was strange.

"Excuse me, Scarlett," said Rachel.

"Can we see the boat from here?"

"Oh, the boat," said Scarlett, rubbing her forehead. "I almost forgot."

They set off again, and soon they saw the river below them. It curved through the jungle like a blue snake.

"There's the landing area," said Kirsty,

peering out of the window on her side.

But Rachel didn't look. She was staring at the back of Aunt Willow's head.

"Kirsty, look," she said. "There's something glowing."

At that moment, Ellen slid down Aunt Willow's hair and landed on Rachel's lap with a little bump. The girls could see her lips moving, but they couldn't hear her voice because of the roaring aeroplane. Ellen fluttered up and tapped their ears with her wand. Suddenly, they could hear her voice loud and clear.

"That's better," she

said. "Oh, girls, I really need your help. Jack Frost is causing chaos in Fairyland! He's used my questing compass to make us muddle up important missions. The Sweet Fairies keep forgetting which candies they are supposed to be taking care of. The Rainbow Fairies are getting their colours mixed up, and Samira the Superhero Fairy keeps forgetting who she's supposed to be saving. Please will you come to Fairyland and help me to stop him?"

"Of course we will," said Kirsty at once.

They knew that they didn't have to worry about being missed. Fairy magic meant that time would stand still in the human world while they were in Fairyland. No one on the plane would notice a thing.

Ellen waved her wand, and Rachel and Kirsty were scooped up in a soft cloud of sparkling fairy dust. The noise of the plane faded, and they felt themselves

shrinking to fairy size. Then the plane
disappeared, and they landed on a hill
among toadstool houses.

"We're in Fairyland," sad Kirsty.

Something was wrong. The toadstool
houses were brown. The grass was red,

and the daisies were blue.

"Oh dear, things are getting worse," said Ellen with a groan.

They landed on the red grass and looked around. Fairies were dashing in all directions, looking upset and confused.

"I can't remember what animal I'm supposed to look after," cried Lauren the Puppy Fairy.

"I've forgotten my special sweet recipe!" Layla the Candyfloss Fairy was wailing.

"Oh my goodness," said Rachel, as Mariana the Goldilocks Fairy fluttered past wearing a Cinderella costume. "If the fairies can't remember what their jobs are, how are we going to remember that we need to get the compass back? What if Jack Frost uses its magic to make us forget our mission?"

Chapter Eight:
Protect the King and Queen

"I know what we could do," said Kirsty suddenly. "My mum always writes messages on her hand when she needs to remember something. Let's all write 'Get the questing compass from Jack Frost' on our hands. Then we just have to help each other remember."

"Great idea, Kirsty," said Ellen.

Rachel found a pen in her pocket and each of them wrote the message. Then Samira the Superhero Fairy sprinted past, tripped and somersaulted into a toadstool house.

"Ouch!" she said. "Hello, Rachel and Kirsty. Thank goodness you're here. I've forgotten how to fly! I can usually fly, right?"

"Yes," said Kirsty. "Oh dear, this is terrible. Samira, have you seen Jack Frost?"

"I was just following him when I saw you," said Samira. "He was heading towards the Fairyland Palace, but he was going too fast for me. It's all up to you now. I can't catch him if I can't fly. You have to stop him from reaching the king and queen. He's planning to get the goblins to tell them that he is the rightful ruler of Fairyland."

"That would be the biggest disaster ever," said Kirsty. "We have to stop him before he makes the king and queen forget who they are."

"Hurry," said Samira. "If anyone can do it, you can!"

Rachel, Kirsty and Ellen zoomed

towards the Fairyland Palace. When they reached the grounds of the palace they spotted three goblins paddling in the glassy Seeing Pool.

"Come out of there, please," said Ellen, landing beside the pool with her arms folded.

The goblins just splashed water at her and stuck out their tongues.

"You can't stop us," they squawked, and

they pointed towards a nearby tree.

With a shock, Rachel noticed a spiky shadow lurking behind the tree. Then Jack Frost popped out with an unpleasant smile.

"Have you silly little fairies come to talk to me?" he asked. "What a shame your memories are so bad. I bet you can't even remember what you want to say."

He opened his hand and the fairies saw a flat, golden object on his palm.

"The questing compass!" Ellen exclaimed.

Jack Frost touched the compass with the tip of his wand, and suddenly Kirsty's

81

thoughts started to get
foggy. She looked at
Rachel, and saw that
her best friend looked
confused.

"What are
we doing here?"
Rachel asked.

Jack Frost cackled,
and the goblins capered
around in glee. But Ellen took Kirsty's
hand and looked at the words she had
written there.

"Get the questing compass from Jack
Frost," she read out loud.

When they heard the words, Rachel
and Kirsty felt their minds clear.

"Give Ellen back the questing compass,"
said Rachel. "It doesn't belong to you."

"We have to warn the king and queen," said Kirsty.

Jack Frost touched the compass with his wand again, and Ellen frowned.

"Warn them about what?" she asked.

Rachel quickly showed Ellen the writing on her hand.

"About how Jack Frost wants to make them forget everything," she said. "But we're not going to let that happen and we won't let him confuse us."

Ellen smiled, and Kirsty had an idea.

"Maybe that's it," she said. "If we can confuse the goblins enough, it might stop them from telling lies to the king and queen. We need to make their brains too dizzy to think straight!"

Holding hands, the fairies darted above the goblins, staying just out of their reach. They zoomed around in a circle, and the goblins watched them, their heads going round and round too.

"Stop staring at them," roared Jack
Frost. "Take your eyes off them!"

But the goblins weren't listening.

"My legs are wobbly," squealed the
tallest one.

"I feel dizzy," wailed
another. "My brain hurts."

"Get away from my
goblins," Jack Frost snarled.

"We won't give up until
you return the questing
compass," said Rachel.

Jack Frost stomped
towards the palace, but the
fairies zipped away from
the goblins and landed in
front of him.

"You flying pests are so annoying," he

snapped. "I'll come back for my treasure when it's not so crowded around here."

He clicked his fingers and the goblins staggered to his side.

"We're going somewhere you won't find us," Jack Frost said, jabbing his finger at the fairies.

There was a flash of blue lightning, and he disappeared with all the goblins.

Chapter Nine:
Fog on the River

Ellen instantly waved her wand, and the girls were back in the noisy, bumpy plane. They were about to land. Ellen fluttered into Kirsty's pocket as the plane flew lower. With three bumps and a bounce, they were on the ground.

"You can see the river to your left," said Scarlett. "Oh! There's a boat."

"Why does she sound surprised?" asked Kirsty.

"It must be because the questing compass is still missing," said Rachel. "It's making everyone forget what they're supposed to be doing."

"Goodness me, that's the *Jenny Jay*," said Aunt Willow in an astonished voice. "It's my friend Nell's boat. What is she doing here?"

"I think we're supposed to meet her, remember, Aunt Willow?" said Rachel.

Aunt Willow frowned and rubbed her forehead.

"That's right," she said. "We're meeting
Nell for ... for ... a fun boat ride?"

"To search for the Lost City," said
Kirsty.

Everyone got off the plane and said
goodbye to Scarlett. A white-haired
woman was standing on the deck of the
boat, and she smiled and beckoned them
towards her.

"Welcome to the *Jenny Jay*," she said.
"Come aboard."

"How exciting it will be to travel
through the jungle in a boat," said Mrs
Walker.

"Thank you for helping me out on this expedition, Nell," said Aunt Willow.

"That's what friends are for," said Nell.

Just then, she started to look confused. It was an expression that Rachel and Kirsty were starting to recognise. It meant that Nell's thoughts were getting foggy.

"Just remind me what this expedition is for," she said.

Aunt Willow took out the piece of paper where she had written all the details of the journey.

"We're going to use an ancient map to find the Lost City," said Aunt Willow. "Nell, you're going to take us down the river to the landing place. From there, we will trek through the mountains, following the clues on the map."

"Yes, of course," said Nell. "How could I have forgotten?"

Soon the *Jenny Jay* was chugging along the river. Rachel, Kirsty and the Walkers leaned over the side of the boat, gazing at the swirling water. The banks of the river were muddy, and every now and then the passengers saw a dark shape slipping into the water.

"Crocodiles," said Mr Walker, rubbing his hands together. "Isn't it wonderful to see them in the wild?"

The journey went slowly. Nell kept forgetting that they were supposed to be going to the landing place, and taking the boat up little inlets instead. Luckily, she had written the route down, so she kept checking her own words and getting back on the right course.

"Let's go and explore the rest of the boat," said Kirsty.

94

They climbed
down a narrow
ladder to the lower
deck. There was a
long corridor with
cabins on either
side. Suddenly,
they heard a loud
groan.

"It came from in
there," said Rachel,
pointing to the
nearest cabin.

They peeped
around the door and saw a goblin sitting
on the floor under a porthole. He was
clutching his tummy with one hand, and
his other hand was over his mouth. He
looked greener than the girls had ever

seen a goblin look. Ellen flew out of
Kirsty's pocket.

"Look in his lap," she exclaimed. "He's
got my questing compass!"

Chapter Ten:
A Little Help
from a Crocodile

The goblin groaned again, and the girls
hurried into the cabin.

"What's wrong?" asked Kirsty.

"Jack Frost told me to stay here so this
thing could keep human heads foggy,"
said the goblin in a shaky voice. "But

then the silly boat started going up
and down and round and round. I feel
poorly."

Kirsty put her arm around his shoulders.

"You're travel sick," she said. "Ellen, can
you help him?"

Ellen was already waving her wand.

The goblin instantly
looked better. He
stood up and took
a deep breath.

"Well done,"
said Rachel.
"Now, what were
we doing down here?"

Kirsty frowned. "I can't
quite remember ..."

The goblin sniggered, but then Rachel
glanced down and saw the words on her
hand.

"'Get the questing compass from Jack
Frost'," she whispered. "Kirsty, Ellen, we
have to keep remembering."

Kirsty touched the goblin's arm.

"Ellen made you feel better,' she said.
"Giving back her questing compass

99

would be a good way to say thank you."

"Blah blah blah," sneered the goblin. "I didn't ask her to help me."

THUNK! The boat bumped into something and everyone rushed over to the porthole.

"We hit the bank," said Rachel. "Nell must have forgotten where we were going again."

"M-m-monster!" cried the goblin.

He pointed through the window and the girls saw a long, scaly crocodile sliding lazily into the water. The goblin stumbled backwards, hugging himself and trembling.

"I want to go home," he wailed.

"Ellen could send you back to Goblin Grotto," said Rachel in a quiet voice.

"I could, in the blink of an eye, if I had my questing compass," said Ellen. "Without it, I can't be sure that my spells will be right. If I felt foggy halfway through, I might send you to Timbuktu by mistake."

The goblin chewed his lip.

"Jack Frost will be cross," he whispered.
"He wants us all to help him find
treasure."

Just then, Rachel glimpsed another
crocodile through the window.

"Oh wow, a crocodile," she said. "Are
we on a wildlife expedition?"

"No more monsters!" said the goblin in a squeaky voice.

He threw the compass at Kirsty, who caught it and stared at it in confusion.

"I think I've seen this before," she said, her head feeling foggy.

Ellen fluttered down and reached out to stroke it.

"It's beautiful," she said.

As soon as her finger touched the compass, it shrank to fairy size. Instantly, Rachel and Kirsty felt

their heads clear. The boat turned and chugged on along the river.

"Nell must have remembered where she was meant to be going," said Rachel.

Ellen gave a
beaming smile and
the frightened goblin
disappeared with
a flick of her
wand.

"He's back
in Goblin
Grotto, safe
on dry land,"
she said. "Now
it's time for me to
take the questing
compass home to
Fairyland. Thank
you for helping
me to find it."

"You're
welcome," said

Rachel. "I hope we can help you find the mighty magnifying glass too."

"I'll see you both again soon," Ellen promised the girls.

She disappeared in a flurry of magical sparkles, and Kirsty and Rachel gave each other a big hug.

"I hope we'll be able to find the mighty magnifying glass in time," said Kirsty.

"We have to," said Rachel. "Without it, Aunt Willow won't be able to see things clearly on the trek."

Just then, they heard Margot's voice.

"Rachel, Kirsty, we're almost at the landing place," she called. "Come up to the top deck – you can see the mountains where we're going to trek to the Lost City."

Feeling a sudden quiver of excitement,

the girls smiled at each other.

"Time for the last stage of our adventure," said Rachel. "Race you to the top deck!"

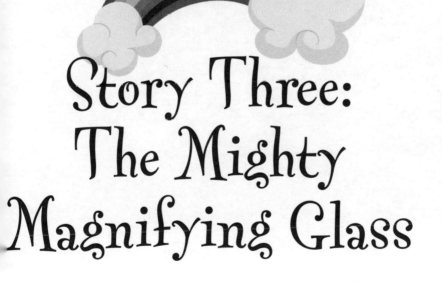

Story Three:
The Mighty
Magnifying Glass

Chapter Eleven:
The Lion, the Eagle and the Star

Nell moored the *Jenny Jay* at the landing place and helped everyone to step off the boat.

"This is going to be such an exciting journey," said Aunt Willow, her eyes sparkling. "We'll find the Lost City and then camp there under the stars."

Everyone pulled on their walking shoes

and checked that they had fresh water
and food in their rucksacks. Aunt Willow
unfolded her map and pointed to a path
that led through some thick leafy plants.

"This is the start of the path," she said.

"Will it take a long time to get there?"
Kirsty asked as they set off.

"I don't think so," said Aunt Willow,
studying the map. "It's well hidden, but
it's not far. Keep an eye out for markers –
signs that will make sure we stay on the
right path. The first marker looks like a
lion. Everyone, keep your eyes peeled for

anything that might look like a lion ... or
might have looked like a lion hundreds
of years ago. Remember, this city hasn't
been visited for a very long time."

The path sloped upwards towards the
distant blue mountains. They tramped
on, looking all around for anything that
might look like a lion. Then suddenly,
Rachel saw it. A huge stone was standing
where the path split in two. It looked as if
it had paws, and the top of it was shaped
like the head of a huge cat.

"It's here!" she cried. "Look – a lion."

Everyone else gathered around the stone.

"I don't see it," said Margot, putting her head on one side.

"It looks more like a kitten to me," said Mr Walker.

Aunt Willow and Mrs Walker shook their heads.

"It's definitely a lion," said Kirsty.

"Can we give it a try?" said Rachel. "Please? We can always turn back if I'm wrong."

After a little hesitation, the grown-ups agreed. They all headed along the right-hand path.

"Next we have to find an eagle," said Aunt Willow, checking her map again.

This time it was Kirsty who spotted the marker. A picture of an eagle was carved

into a rock, heading down an overgrown track.

"That looks more like a butterfly than an eagle," said Mrs Walker.

"Besides, the track is too overgrown," said Mr Walker. "It can't be the right way."

The grown-ups walked past the track, and the girls had to follow.

"It didn't look anything like a butterfly," said Rachel in a low voice. "Why couldn't they see it?"

"Could it be because of the mighty magnifying glass?" said Kirsty. "Ellen told us that it helps people to see things clearly. Maybe it being missing is stopping the others from seeing the markers."

"I wonder why we are still able to see clearly," said Rachel.

They walked on up the mountain for a while, but all the stones were smooth and there was no sign of an eagle shape.

"Let's go back and check Kirsty's eagle," said Aunt Willow eventually. "I don't know why we didn't at least try it. I usually check every clue."

Smiling, Kirsty and Rachel led the

way back to the eagle. They went down the narrow track in single file. It opened out after a little way, and they saw that they were walking on an ancient brick path. Weeds and grasses had pushed up between the bricks.

"Even if this isn't the right path, it is fascinating," said Aunt Willow, snapping some photos. "Keep a lookout for a star shape – that's the next marker."

Rachel and Kirsty were in front when they saw a flash of colour where the path split ahead. They ran forwards and kneeled down.

"It's a star," said Rachel. "Look, it's made of little coloured stones."

"They're all set into the bricks," said Kirsty. "We've found it!"

Aunt Willow, Margot, and Mr and Mrs

Walker joined them and peered down at the stones.

"That's a circle," said Mrs Walker.

"It looks more like a diamond to me," said Margot.

"We can both see it," said Kirsty. "Can we just check down the path in case?"

"Please?" added Rachel, looking at her aunt. "You said you usually check every clue."

Aunt Willow smiled. "You're right," she said. "Let's explore!"

Chapter Twelve:
Ellen Returns

The path was long and narrow. Rachel and Kirsty followed Aunt Willow until they reached a clearing. It was surrounded by a tangle of weeds and plants.

"There's nothing here," said Aunt Willow. "We must have come the wrong way after all."

Kirsty's stomach suddenly gave a loud

rumble, and Margot smiled at her.

"I'm hungry too," she said. "Mum always forgets about stopping for food when she's exploring. I think it's time to have those sandwiches we packed."

Everyone agreed and they found a place to sit. As they unwrapped their sandwiches, Rachel noticed how disappointed Aunt Willow looked.

"Maybe the map is wrong," she said. "I really thought that I was going to find the Lost City."

"You will," said Margot, leaning against her mum.

"I'm sure it's really close by," said Mr Walker.

"We'll find it soon," said Kirsty.

As Rachel and Kirsty were finishing their food, Kirsty saw a light sparkling among the tangle of weeds to their right. She nudged Rachel, who smiled. They both knew what that light meant!

"Is it OK if we go and explore?" she asked.

"Of course," said Mrs Walker. "That's what we're here for. But don't go too far."

The girls walked around behind the tangle of weeds and saw Ellen waiting for them, leaning against a rock. She jumped forwards

when she saw them.

"I'm so glad to see you, Ellen," said Kirsty. "No one else seems to be seeing things the same way we are."

"It's because Jack Frost has my mighty magnifying glass," said Ellen. "It helps people to see clearly. Without it, they can't see things as they truly are."

"Why are Kirsty and I still able to see things as they are?" asked Rachel.

Ellen fluttered up and touched Rachel's

locket with the tip of her finger. Queen Titania had given one to her and one to Kirsty, and they were filled with fairy dust.

"The fairy dust has given you extra strength," said Ellen. "The magic of your friendship gives you strength too. But the closer you get to Jack Frost and the magnifying glass, the more difficult it has become for you to see things as they are. It's the same for me."

"What do you mean?" said Kirsty. "Are we getting close to where Jack Frost is hiding?"

"Look around," said Ellen. "We are in the Lost City now, but Jack Frost has used the magic of the magnifying glass

to make it look like something else. Until we get it back from him, no one but Jack Frost and the goblins will be able to see the Lost City as it truly is."

"Do you mean that Jack Frost and his goblins are right here?" asked Rachel.

"I'm sure they are," said Ellen. "The magnifying glass is helping to keep them hidden."

Just then, Kirsty heard a faint noise. She knew what it was at once.

"You're right," she said to Ellen. "I've just heard a goblin sniggering somewhere close by. I think they must be disguised as something else!"

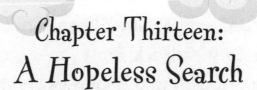

Chapter Thirteen:
A Hopeless Search

"We have to make them show us where they really are," said Ellen. "But how?"

"I've got an idea," said Rachel. She gave Kirsty and Ellen a wink and then started talking in a loud voice. "I'm finally starting to realise how clever the goblins really are," she said.

There were a few whispered squawks

nearby, but it was hard to tell where the sounds were coming from.

"Me too," said Kirsty. "They shouldn't have to do what Jack Frost says."

"She's right," said a goblin in a squeaky voice.

"We should be in charge," said another goblin, getting louder.

"Close your eyes," whispered Ellen suddenly. "The mighty magnifying glass is stopping us from seeing things as they really are. We have to trust our other senses instead. If we can't see, we can't be tricked."

Rachel and Kirsty closed their eyes and listened. The goblin voices seemed to get louder.

"The sound's coming from the left," Rachel murmured.

She reached out her arms and felt her way forwards.

"They'll never catch us," a goblin said, cackling.

Kirsty stretched out her fingertips and brushed against something knobbly.

"We've got the better of the pesky humans this time," said another.

Rachel and Kirsty threw their arms around where they thought the sound was coming from, and then opened their eyes.

"We're holding trees," said Kirsty in surprise.

Both girls had their arms wrapped around green-leaved saplings.

"Don't let go,"

cried Ellen. "Keep holding on and blink hard. The trees might not be real."

Feeling confused, the girls did as she said, blinking as hard and fast as they could. Suddenly, the trees shimmered like the Seeing Pool in Fairyland, and Rachel and Kirsty saw that they had their arms around two goblins.

"Keep quiet and they'll never know they've got us," hissed the first goblin out of the corner of his mouth.

"Tee-hee!" said the second goblin. "Ho ho! Ha ha! This one's tickling my armpits."

"We can see you," said Kirsty, letting him go.

"Help!" wailed the goblin. "What do you want? Leave us alone."

"We will," said Rachel, keeping her arms around the other goblin. "As soon as you give back the mighty magnifying glass."

"We can't give it back," the goblin squawked, struggling to get free. "We don't have it."

"Tell us where it is, then," said Ellen, flying down to hover in front of him.

"Fairies too," the goblin cried. "Why can we never get away from you bothersome little creatures?"

"Because you are always following Jack Frost's orders," said Rachel.

"Yes, and he's much too clever for you," the goblin retorted, sticking out his tongue. "His disguise is brilliant and you'll never see through it. He wants us

to look for treasure, and we're going to
do exactly what he said."

He tore himself away from her and
both goblins scampered off. The girls
started to chase them, but Ellen shook
her head.

"Let them go," she said. "Jack Frost
doesn't understand. There's no treasure
hidden in the Lost City – the treasure is
the ruined city itself. Any true explorer
would think it was worth more than a
rucksack full of diamonds to discover this
place."

Rachel and Kirsty started to search for
Jack Frost with Ellen fluttering between
them. They peered under bushes and up
trees. They checked behind huge, mossy
boulders and waded through a muddy
hollow. They walked around a cactus that

had two prickly bulges dipped in a pool of water.

"That cactus looks as if it's cooling its arms in the water," said Rachel.

There were all sorts of wonderful plants to see, but there was no sign of Jack Frost or the mighty magnifying glass.

"It's hopeless," said Ellen, her wings drooping. "The goblins were right. Jack Frost's disguise is so brilliant that we can't see through it!"

Chapter Fourteen:
The Magic of Friendship

"No," said Kirsty with sudden excitement. "Ellen, don't give up hope. Do you remember what you said about our extra strength?"

"Of course," said Ellen. "I said that it comes from fairy dust and the magic of your friendship."

"Maybe we can use that strength now,"

said Kirsty. "Rachel, hold my hand. We have to give each other the strength to see clearly."

The best friends held hands and stared into each other's eyes.

"See clearly," said Rachel, focusing on her best friend with all her might.

"I'm thinking about the magic of our friendship. I'm thinking about Rainspell Island and all the wonderful adventures we've shared."

"See clearly," repeated Kirsty. "I'm thinking about the magic of our lockets. I'm thinking about growing fairy wings and travelling to Fairyland in a flurry of fairy dust."

Suddenly, a crystal-clear picture popped into Rachel's head. It was a picture of the cactus they had passed earlier.

"That cactus looked just as if it had arms," she remembered.

A picture pinged into Kirsty's head too.

"The pool is shiny and reflective, just like glass," she said.

They turned and ran back to the cactus and the pool.

"Be careful," said Ellen. "Those cactus prickles look sharp."

"I trust the magic of our friendship," said Kirsty, reaching out to touch the plant. "I don't believe that this is a cactus at all."

As soon as her fingertips brushed against the spikes, the plant shimmered. The prickly bulges became bony arms. The green stem became a blue cloak, and the bumpy top of the plant became a spiky head.

"You interfering little snoops!" someone shouted.

"It's Jack Frost!" Rachel exclaimed. "And look what

he's holding," Kirsty added.

Now they could see that the shiny pool was really a golden magnifying glass.

Both girls reached out and grabbed it, holding on as tightly as they could. Jack Frost bared his teeth.

"Let go!" he growled.

The girls shook their heads and clung

on even more tightly. Jack Frost tugged
at the magnifying glass. Then he spotted
Ellen, who perched on Rachel's shoulder.

"You," he hissed through gritted teeth.
"This thing is rubbish. It hasn't shown
me any treasure! Tell me how to make it
work."

"It's working just fine," said Ellen,
folding her arms.

"Fibber," Jack Frost snapped.

He yanked the magnifying glass
suddenly, and the girls lost their hold on
it. He hugged it to his chest.

"Fairies don't tell fibs," said Ellen. "The
mighty magnifying glass doesn't lead
the way to lost treasure – none of my
magical objects will do that."

"I don't believe you," said Jack Frost.
"What's the point of being an explorer

if you can't find gold and jewels and be rich and famous?"

"I don't expect you to understand," Ellen said. "We explore for the love of discovery. All the best and happiest explorers go on expeditions and quests for the thrill of the adventure, not for treasure."

"But I heard the humans talking about a priceless treasure," Jack Frost said with a crafty expression. "You're trying to trick me."

"They were talking about the Lost City itself," said Ellen. "It's worth more than riches or fame. It connects human beings to their past and teaches them about their world."

Jack Frost curled his lip.

"I'd rather have a bag of gold than a

pile of crumbling stones in the middle of the jungle," he muttered.

"That's because you don't have the heart of an explorer," said Ellen. "The mighty magnifying glass is useless to you. It will lead you to great treasure, but you won't understand the value of it. The mighty magnifying glass won't give you what you want."

"I don't believe a word you're saying,"

Jack Frost retorted, backing away from them. "You just want the treasure for yourself. I'll never give the magnifying glass back. It's mine!"

Chapter Fifteen:
Lost and Found

"Ellen is telling you the truth," said
Kirsty.

"Look around," said Ellen. "If there
were gold here, you would see it."

Jack Frost glanced around. When he
spoke again, his voice was very quiet.

"Are you telling me that I've wasted all

this time on things that won't even lead
me to treasure?" he said.

Ellen nodded, and he stared at her for a
moment. Then he opened his mouth and
let out a bellow of rage. He stamped his
foot and let go of the magnifying glass to
shake both his fists at the little fairy.

"Quick!" said Rachel.

She and Kirsty darted forwards, and
Ellen swooped after them. As soon as
she reached down to take the mighty
magnifying glass, it shrank back to fairy
size. Jack Frost let out a howl of rage.

"I've had enough of meddling humans

and pesky fairies," he yelled. "I'm going to think of another way to get treasure, and next time, no one's going to stop me!"

He stamped his foot and disappeared in a clap of thunder.

"I don't think he'll be coming back here," said Rachel.

"No," Ellen agreed with a grin. "I think he's had enough of being an explorer!"

She turned a happy somersault in mid-air. Rachel

and Kirsty held hands and spun around,
faster and faster, until they lost their grip
and fell down on the grass, laughing
and breathless. Ellen fluttered down and
landed on Kirsty's knee.

"Thank you both for everything you've done," she said. "As soon as I get the mighty magnifying glass back where it belongs, everyone will be able to see clearly again."

"It was our pleasure to help," said Kirsty. "Sharing our adventure with you made it even more exciting."

Ellen smiled and waved her wand. With
a dazzling flash of fairy dust, she was
gone. Rachel jumped up.

"Come on," she said. "Let's go and find
the others."

The girls ran back to where everyone
else was finishing their picnic. As they
helped to tidy up, Aunt Willow gave an
exclamation.

"I don't know why I didn't see it
before," she said. "Look around."

Rachel and Kirsty gazed around and
saw that the tangled weeds seemed
less dense than before. Suddenly they
could see that the mossy boulders were
crumbling walls, carved with intricate
patterns. The muddy hollow was a vast
sunken chamber with a mosaic floor.
Broken arches leaned against trees, and

ancient carvings could be glimpsed behind tangled brambles. Gasping in delight, Aunt Willow leaped to her feet.

"This is the place of my dreams," she said.

She darted around, uttering cries of delight over each new thing she found. Rachel and Kirsty watched her for a few minutes, but then they couldn't resist exploring themselves. Soon everyone was delving into the heart of the Lost City.

"It's an amazing feeling to think that we are the first people to walk through this place for hundreds of years," said Margot. "It feels full of mysteries and memories."

"This city will tell us so much about the people who once lived here," said Aunt Willow. "I can't wait to come back

here with an archaeological team and the right equipment to help us preserve it."

"We're lucky to have been with you for the discovery," said Mr Walker, putting his arm around his sister's shoulders.

They set up their camp for the night
among the ruined walls of the Lost City.
As the stars shone down and the campfire
glowed, Mrs Walker asked Aunt Willow to
tell them about some of her most exciting
expeditions. Aunt Willow laughed and her
eyes sparkled.

"I've certainly had a few adventures," she said. "But nothing as wonderful as finding this magical place."

Rachel and Kirsty smiled at each other as they cuddled up under a blanket.

"I think this has to be one of the most magical adventures we've ever had, too," Kirsty whispered. "And that really is saying something!"

The End

Now it's time for Kirsty and Rachel to help...

Cara the Coding Fairy

Read on for a sneak peek ...

"We're here!" said Rachel Walker, undoing her seatbelt and smiling at her best friend, Kirsty Tate.

Rachel and Kirsty had been looking forward to the coding convention Funcode for weeks. The organiser, Professor Stark, was an old school friend of Mr Walker's. He had sent the girls two tickets to the convention so that they could brush up their skills and learn the latest programming methods.

"I'm sorry we're a bit late," said Mr

Walker, checking his watch.

"That's OK," said Rachel. "It's easy to get lost in the city."

The best friends jumped out of Mr Walker's car and looked up at the city conference centre.

"Oh my goodness, this place is huge," said Kirsty.

"I think the whole of Wetherbury village would fit inside," said Rachel with a laugh.

Calling all parents, carers and teachers!
The Rainbow Magic fairies are here to help
your child enter the magical world of reading.
Whatever reading stage they are at, there's
a Rainbow Magic book for everyone!
Here is Lydia the Reading Fairy's guide to
supporting your child's journey at all levels.

Starting Out

Our Rainbow Magic Beginner Readers are perfect for first-time readers who are just beginning to develop reading skills and confidence. Approved by teachers, they contain a full range of educational levelling, as well as lively full-colour illustrations.

1

Developing Readers

Rainbow Magic Early Readers contain longer stories and wider vocabulary for building stamina and growing confidence. These are adaptations of our most popular Rainbow Magic stories, specially developed for younger readers in conjunction with an Early Years reading consultant, with full-colour illustrations.

2

Going Solo

The Rainbow Magic chapter books - a mixture of series and one-off specials - contain accessible writing to encourage your child to venture into reading independently. These highly collectible and much-loved magical stories inspire a love of reading to last a lifetime.

3

www.rainbowmagicbooks.co.uk

"Rainbow Magic got my daughter reading chapter books. Great sparkly covers, cute fairies and traditional stories full of magic that she found impossible to put down" - Mother of Edie (6 years)

"Florence LOVES the Rainbow Magic books. She really enjoys reading now" - Mother of Florence (6 years)

The Rainbow Magic Reading Challenge

Well done, fairy friend – you have completed the book!
This book was worth 10 points.

See how far you have climbed on the
Reading Rainbow opposite.

The more books you read, the more points you will get,
and the closer you will be to becoming a Fairy Princess!

Do you want your own Reading Rainbow?
1. Cut out the coin below
2. Go to the Rainbow Magic website
3. Download and print out your poster
4. Add your coin and climb up the Reading Rainbow!

There's all this and lots more at
www.rainbowmagicbooks.co.uk

You'll find activities, competitions, stories, a special
newsletter and complete profiles of all the
Rainbow Magic fairies. Find a fairy with your name!